STEP INTO READING®

1
STEP
READY TO READ

P9-DMI-184

Panda Kisses

by Alyssa Satin Capucilli

illustrated by Kay Widdowson

Random House New York

Mother Bear,

I want a kiss!

A soft kiss?

A sweet kiss?

A sticky bamboo
treat kiss?

Father Bear,
I want a kiss!

A low kiss?

A high kiss?

A climb up
to the sky kiss?

15

How about a sunny kiss?

How about a bunny kiss?

A fish kiss?

A flower kiss?

Or a cool
sun shower kiss?

What other kisses
can there be?
I must find
the one for me.

A kiss

inside a silk cocoon?

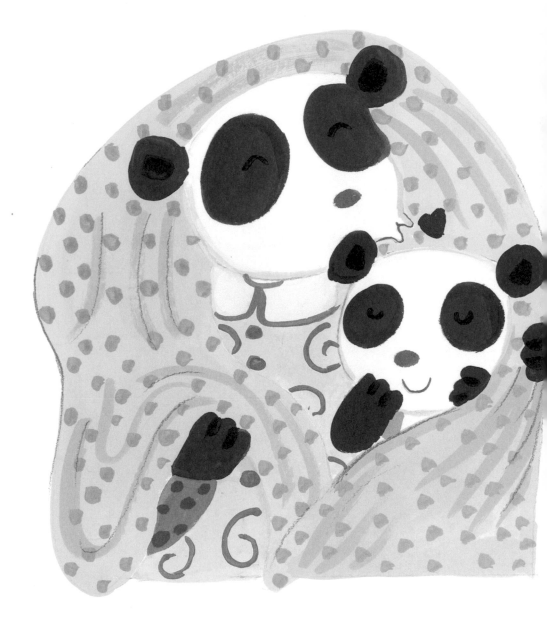

A kiss

under a big full moon?

WAIT!

28

There are many kisses
that will do!

But the best kiss is—
from both of you!